ALL YOU CAN IMAGINE

WRITTEN AND ILLUSTRATED BY
BERNARDO MARÇOLLA

free spirit
PUBLISHING®

Library of Congress Cataloging-in-Publication Data
Names: Marçolla, Bernardo Andrade, 1973- author. | Marçolla, Bernardo Andrade, 1973– illustrator.
Title: All you can imagine / written and illustrated by Bernardo Marçolla.
Description: Minneapolis : Free Spirit Publishing Inc., 2021. | Audience: Ages 5–8
Identifiers: LCCN 2020043124 (print) | LCCN 2020043125 (ebook) | ISBN 9781631986512 (hardcover) | ISBN 9781631986529 (pdf) |
    ISBN 9781631986536 (epub)
Subjects: LCSH: Imagination—Juvenile literature. | Thought and thinking—Juvenile literature.
Classification: LCC BF408 .M23487 2021 (print) | LCC BF408 (ebook) | DDC 153.3—dc23
LC record available at https://lccn.loc.gov/2020043124
LC ebook record available at https://lccn.loc.gov/2020043125

Free Spirit Publishing does not have control over or assume responsibility for author or third-party websites and their content.

Reading Level Grade 3; Interest Level Ages 5–8;
Fountas & Pinnell Guided Reading Level O

Edited by Alison Behnke
Cover and interior design by Shannon Pourciau

10 9 8 7 6 5 4 3 2 1
Printed in China
R18861220

Free Spirit Publishing Inc.
6325 Sandburg Road, Suite 100
Minneapolis, MN 55427-3674
(612) 338-2068
help4kids@freespirit.com
freespirit.com

FSC
www.fsc.org
MIX
Paper from responsible sources
FSC® C144853

Free Spirit offers competitive pricing.
Contact edsales@freespirit.com for pricing information on multiple quantity purchases.

DEDICATION

This book is dedicated to all those, young and old, who through their hearts and efforts use their imaginations to bring harmony and beauty to the world and make it a better place for us all.

ACKNOWLEDGMENTS

My acknowledgment to all the streams of Life, which open our thoughts and hearts to the new and beautiful things that can be created or discovered when we are sufficiently attuned.

My gratitude to the entire Free Spirit Publishing team. To Shannon Pourciau and Amanda Shofner, my thanks for their important participation at different stages of the process. Also, my most special thanks to Meg Bratsch for her openness, which paved the way for the expression and sharing of new ideas—and to Alison Behnke, who contributed generously and significantly to the construction of this book, from its earliest stages to its bloom.

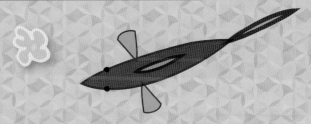

This book will tell
you a secret.

It's about the invisible things
in the universe . . .

... and how *you* can make them visible.

The secret is: **IMAGINATION!**

Imagination is like a vehicle.

You can use it to travel great distances and discover wonderful new ways to look at the universe.

Imagination is what we see with our eyes closed. It is what we dream of and what we wish were real.

You see, there is a world all around you, and there is a world inside of you. Imagination connects the two.

In fact, imagination connects everything, everywhere.

Like water, imagination can look simple on the surface, while at the same time being as rich as the ocean.

Imagination connects what is on the surface with the depths within. It connects things that we may believe are completely separate.

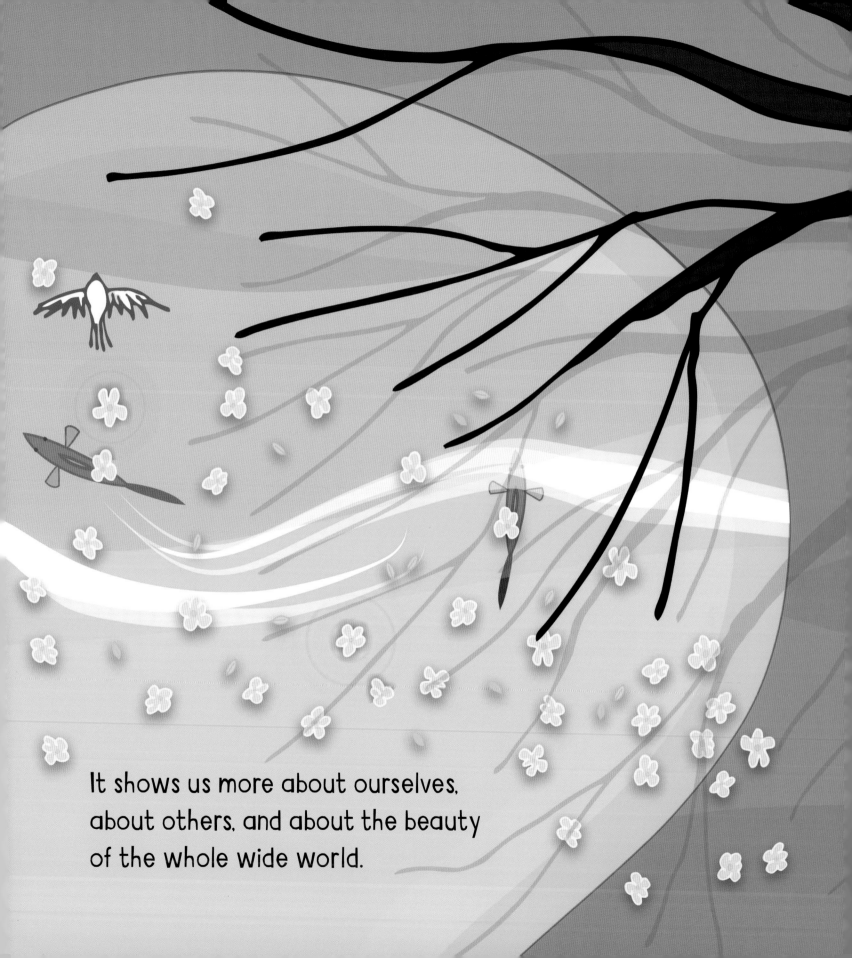

It shows us more about ourselves,
about others, and about the beauty
of the whole wide world.

Imagination is exciting and powerful. But we can't always call up ideas and inspiration whenever we feel like it.

Still, we *can* help them grow and bloom.

To do this we have to open our hearts, our minds, and our eyes to the world around us.

Then we feel that we are part of the whole universe. And just as we breathe in and out, imagination can now flow through us.

When we are in tune with ourselves and with the world, we open the doors of imagination.

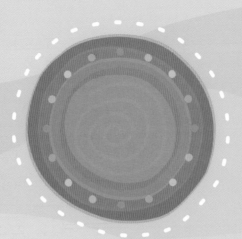

It's no use hurrying.
Imagination takes time.
And it only comes when
it wants. So we wait,
and watch.

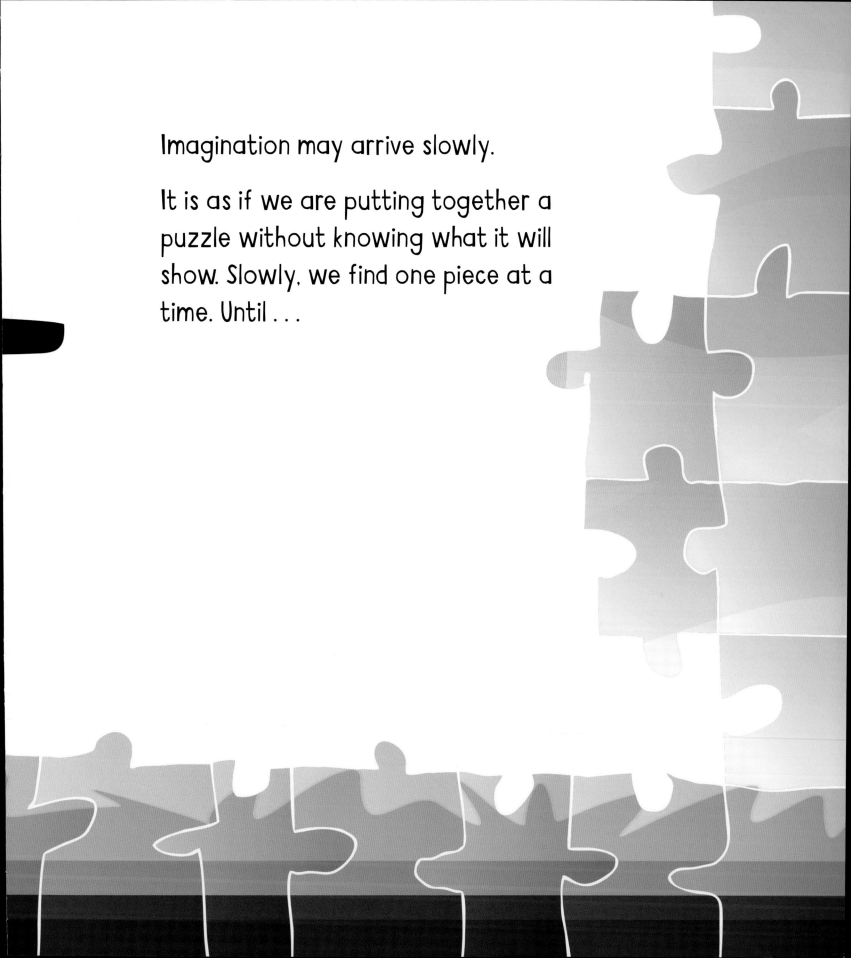

Imagination may arrive slowly.

It is as if we are putting together a puzzle without knowing what it will show. Slowly, we find one piece at a time. Until . . .

. . . something new and beautiful appears.

Or imagination may arrive suddenly.

It is as if we wake up and immediately remember a brilliant idea we dreamed.

This dream idea is like a bird that takes flight. If we don't pay attention, we may lose sight of it. But if we look closely at what we dreamed, we may feel as if we have gained wings of our own.

Imagination can introduce us to something completely original. It can help us discover a whole new world.

And we want to share
what we have seen
with everyone else.

One way to do this is through **ART**.

Art can show others what we saw.
It can even help them feel how we felt.

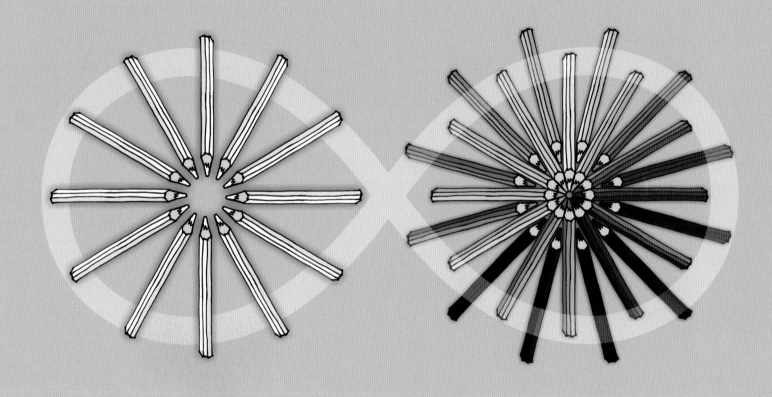

We can write songs, stories, or poems.
We can paint, draw, or take photographs.
We can make crafts.

We can also build things.

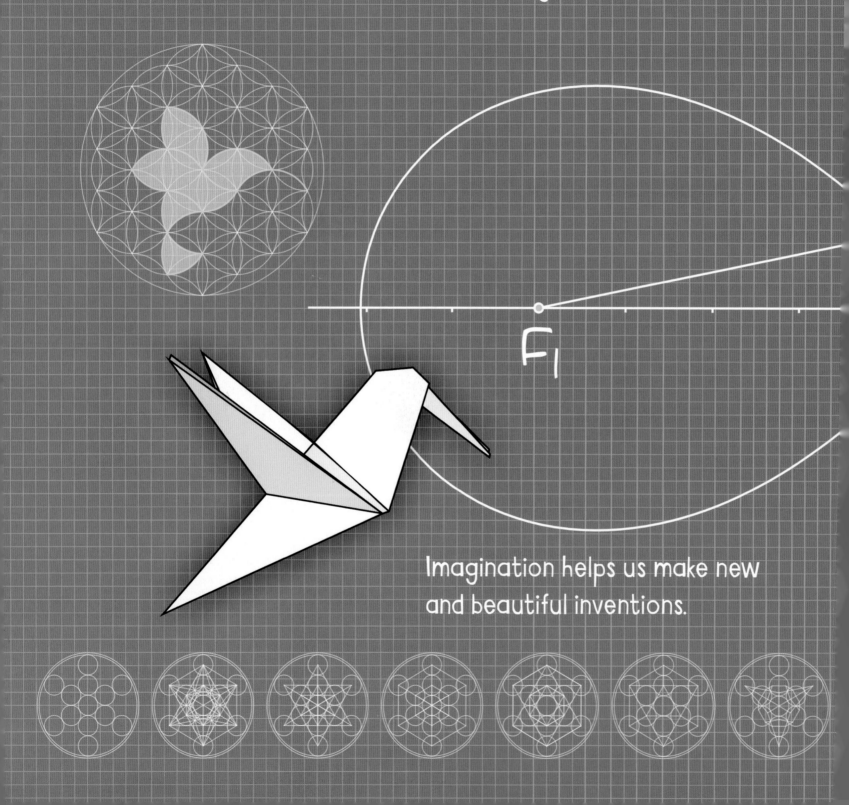

F_1

Imagination helps us make new
and beautiful inventions.

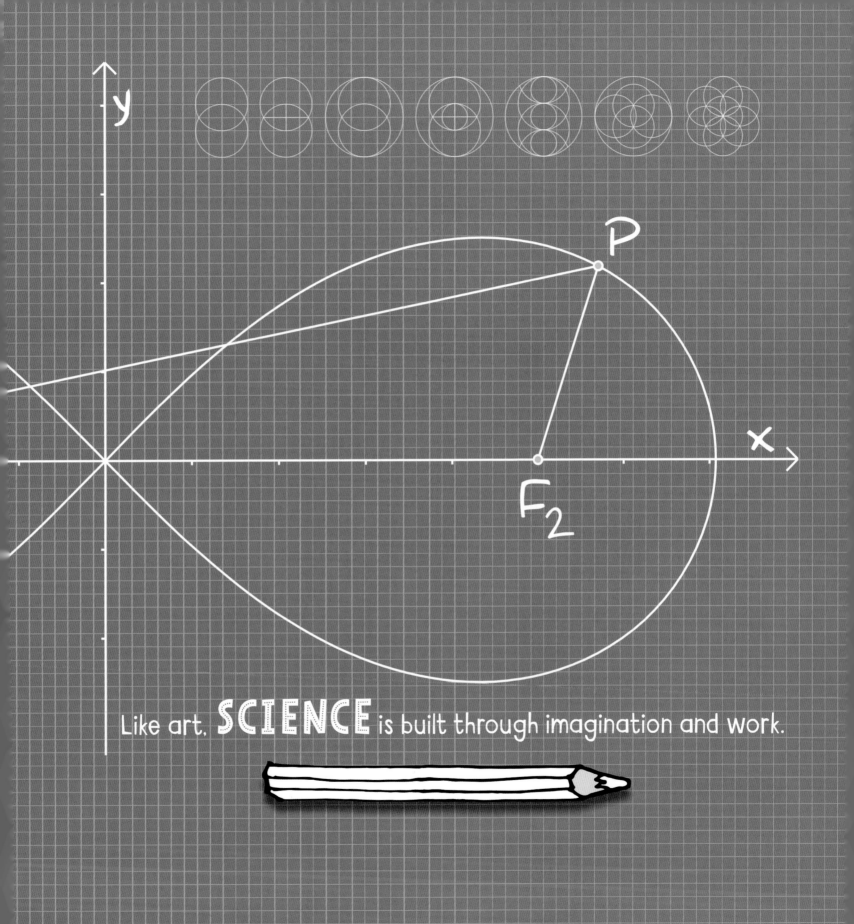

Like art, **SCIENCE** is built through imagination and work.

Here is another secret: When we share what imagination has shown us, we feel closer to everyone else.

We feel more in tune with the universe around us.

And we learn more about our own hearts.

We can do this over and over again.

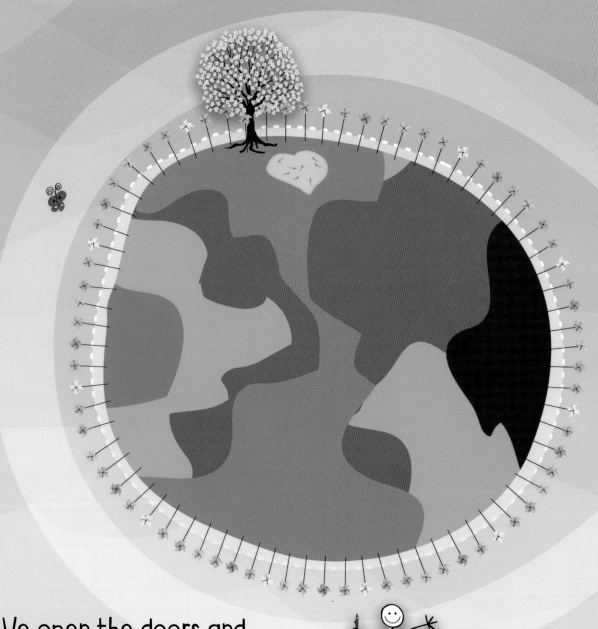

We open the doors and
windows for imagination
to come . . .

...and we share our discoveries with others.

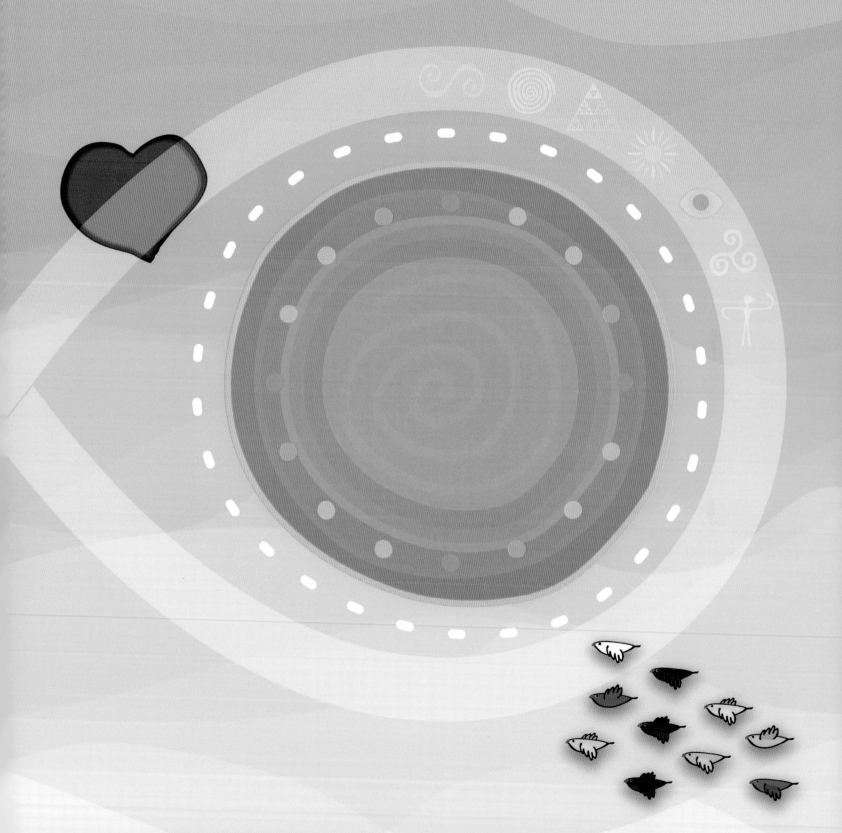

Bit by bit, something wonderful
happens: We fill the world with
everything our imaginations bring.

We are surrounded by
beautiful new images that were
once just pieces of a puzzle . . .

∞

. . . and we see the flight of colorful birds we never knew existed.

A NOTE FROM BERNARDO

At the beginning of this book, I told you that you'd learn a secret. And now that you've read the book, you know what it is: imagination!

When some people think about imagination, they might not believe that it's very important. Some of them might even think it's silly or that it takes us away from reality.

But I think just the opposite. Through imagination, I believe we can see reality even more clearly. Imagination helps us learn more about our own nature, about what makes us human, about the richness of our own mind and spirit.

Imagination often comes from within, and it is a powerful way to understand ourselves. It helps us explore the deeper realities that exist inside each one of us, but that we sometimes forget to pay attention to—especially when we're busy, or distracted, or sad, or worried.

Imagination also seems to come from outside of us. When this happens, we often call it inspiration. Then it helps us understand new things not only about ourselves, but also about the realities, stories, sorrows, hopes, and joys that connect all people everywhere. It can even help us get closer to ideas that remain mysterious to all of us.

When we follow and explore our imagination—and our inspiration—we discover many wonderful things. But these experiences can be difficult to hold, like wild birds that fly away when we get too close. Then we face the challenge of how to capture what we saw, and how to share it. One of the best ways to do this is through art.

Here is another secret: we are all artists! "Art" can sound very grand and important. Sometimes people fear that they cannot create or even appreciate art. But all of us, whether we think of ourselves as artists or not, can share experiences through art. We can feel the sensations that a beautiful melody evokes. We can see beauty and depth in a painting or a sculpture or a quilt or a dance. We can feel a deep connection to the people in a story, a poem, or a song. And we all have something to say through our own creations. The art you make does not have to be like anyone else's. So seek out your own ways to show others what your imagination reveals to you.

As strange as it may seem, science is also an art form. It gains strength and energy from our inventions and our dreams, and makes leaps from our imagination and inspiration. Like other types of art, science requires commitment and hard work to become a reality that we can share with others.

No matter how we choose to share the beauty and wonder we see in our imagination, something amazing happens when we do: We all understand more about each other and ourselves. We all feel more connected to other people and to the whole universe. This connection is powerful! It makes us want to keep sharing, and keep connecting. And so we make more art, more creations, more inventions, and we send those out into the world. This process feeds itself, over and over, in a continuous cycle of infinite imagination.

So, can you already feel imagination flowing through *you*?

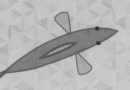

ABOUT THE AUTHOR AND ILLUSTRATOR

BERNARDO MARÇOLLA is an author and illustrator who holds a doctorate and post doctorate in literature, as well as a master's degree in psychology, and who has more than ten years of experience as a professor of psychology. Since 2012, he has been an analyst in the Human Resources area of the Brazilian Institute of Geography and Statistics, and in 2017, he published the book *Psychology and Ecology: Nature, Subjectivity and Its Intersections* (in Portuguese). The ideas in that book inspired him to create his first book for children, *Me and You and the Universe*. He loves chocolate and still has not given up on learning to draw a little better. He lives in Belo Horizonte, Brazil, with his wife and two cats—and they are already planning for a third cat.

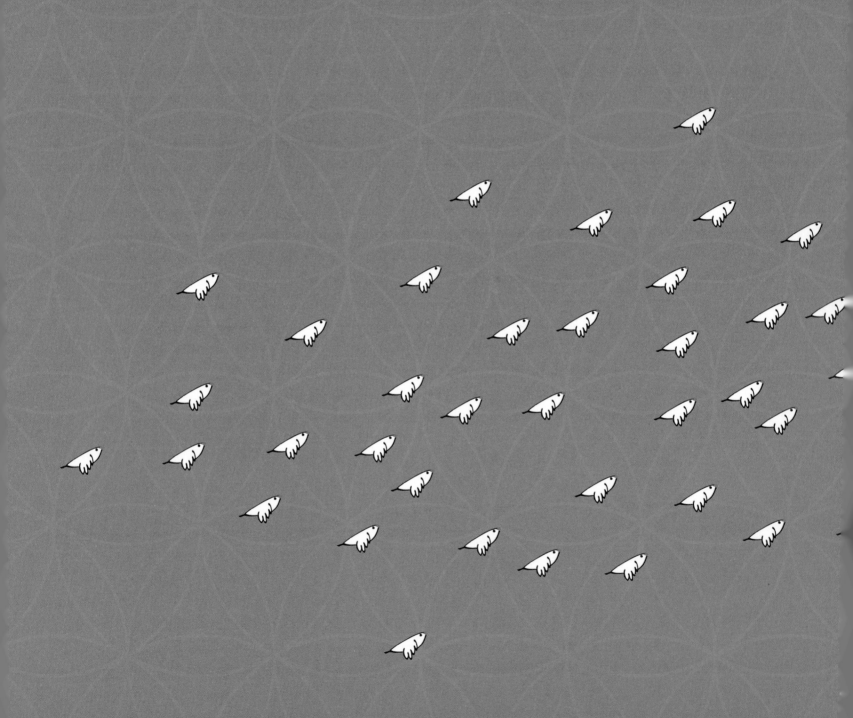